Phonics Focus: long a (eigh)

THE SLEIGH

BY CHRISTINA EARLEY

ILLUSTRATED BY
ANASTASIA KLECKNER

A Blue Marlin Book

Introduction:

Phonics is the relationship between letters and sounds. It is the foundation for reading words, or decoding. A phonogram is a letter or group of letters that represents a sound. Students who practice phonics and sight words become fluent word readers. Having word fluency allows students to build their comprehension skills and become skilled and confident readers.

Activities:

BEFORE READING

Use your finger to underline the key phonogram in each word in the *Words to Read* list on page 3. Then, read the word. For longer words, look for ways to break the word into smaller parts (double letters, word I know, ending, etc.).

DURING READING

Use sticky notes to annotate for understanding. Write questions, make connections, summarize each page after it is read, or draw an emoji that describes how you felt about different parts.

AFTER READING

Share and discuss your sticky notes with an adult or peer who also read the story.

Key Word/Phonogram: sleigh

Words to Read:

eight
neigh
freight
sleigh
weighed
bobsleigh
eightvo
eighty
flyweight
lightweight
neighbors
unweights
weightless
weighty
counterweights
heavyweights
underweight

Eighty reindeer are getting ready for the Sleigh Pulling tryouts.

Only eight will be chosen to be on Santa's Sleigh Team this year.

SANTA'S
SLEIGH
TEAM
?
?
?
?
?
?
?
?

First, each reindeer is weighed.

Runner and Skye are in the flyweight group. Snow and Ice get put in the lightweight group. The heavyweights are Candy Cane and Tiny.

Many others are underweight. They do not make it to the next round.

FLYWEIGHT
RUNNER
SKYE
SNOW
TINY

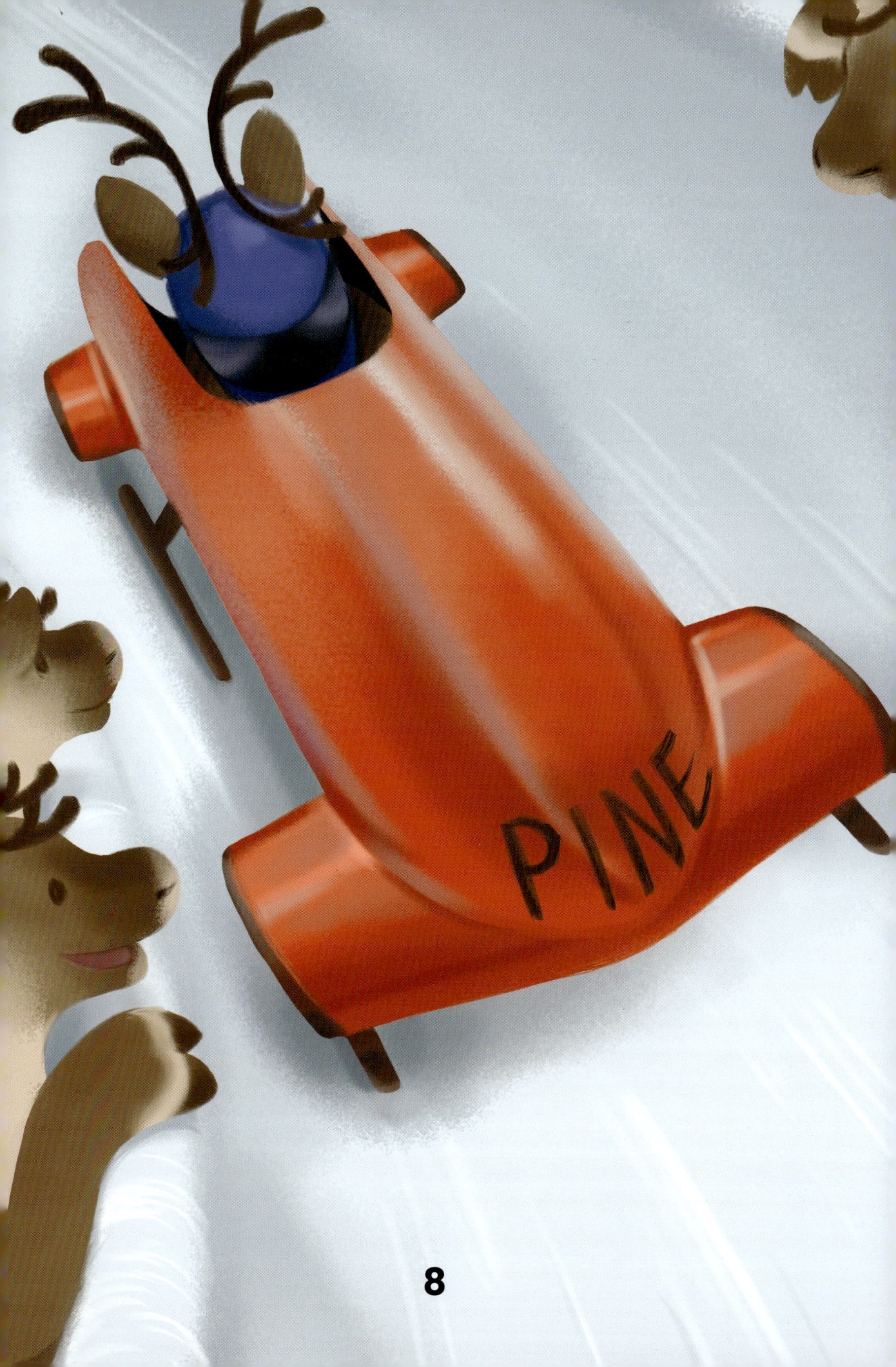
PINE

The bobsleigh test is next.

Pine unweights the left ski of the bobsleigh to make a fast turn.

The reindeer watching neigh with joy!

Santa has a weighty choice to make.

He folds paper three times to make an eightvo book. There is a name on each page!

The lucky reindeer are joined to the sleigh in pairs as counterweights.

The sleigh looks weightless as it flies away with its freight of toys.

North Pole neighbors cheer off the team!

Quiz:

1. **True or false?** Eighteen reindeer will be chosen for the team.
2. **True or false?** Runner and Skye are the heaviest reindeer.
3. **True or false?** Santa balances the sleigh by attaching the reindeer in pairs.
4. Do you think having tryouts is a good way to choose the best reindeer to pull the sleigh? Use details from the story to support your answer.
5. What is the genre of this book? How do you know?

Flip the book around for answers!

Answers:

1. False
2. False
3. True
4. Possible answers: Yes, because the reindeer need to be the right weight and need to be able to pull the sleigh.
   No, because the reindeer only need magic to fly.
5. It is fiction because it is about made-up people, animals, and events.

Activities:

1. Write a story about what happens after the sleigh leaves the North Pole.

2. Write a new story using some or all of the "eigh" words from this book.

3. Create a vocabulary word map for a word that was new to you. Write the word in the middle of a paper. Surround it with a definition, illustration, sentence, and other words related to the vocabulary word.

4. Make a song to help others learn the long a sound of "eigh."

5. Design a game to practice reading and spelling words with "eigh."

Written by: Christina Earley
Illustrated by: Anastasia Kleckner
Design by: Rhea Magaro-Wallace
Editor: Kim Thompson
Educational Consultant: Marie Lemke, M.Ed.
Series Development: James Earley

Library of Congress PCN Data
The Sleigh (eigh) / Christina Earley
Blue Marlin Readers
ISBN 978-1-6389-7996-8 (hard cover)
ISBN 979-8-8873-5055-4 (paperback)
ISBN 979-8-8873-5114-8 (EPUB)
ISBN 979-8-8873-5173-5 (eBook)
Library of Congress Control Number: 2022944997

Printed in China.

Seahorse Publishing Company
seahorsepub.com

Copyright © 2023 **SEAHORSE PUBLISHING COMPANY**

All rights reserved. No part of this publication may be reproduced, stored in a retrieval system or be transmitted in any form or by any means, electronic, mechanical, photocopying, recording, or otherwise, without the prior written permission of Seahorse Publishing Company.

Published in the United States
Seahorse Publishing
PO Box 771325
Coral Springs, FL 33077